P9-BYE-807

Donated to the
Massanutten Regional Library

DISCARD

In Memory of

The MORNING CHAIR

by Barbara M. Joosse ❧ Illustrated by Marcia Sewall

MASSANUTTEN REGIONAL LIBRARY
DISCARD

Clarion Books ❧ New York

Easy
JOOSS

Clarion Books
a Houghton Mifflin Company imprint
215 Park Avenue South, New York, NY 10003
Text copyright © 1995 by Barbara M. Joosse
Illustrations copyright © 1995 by Marcia Sewall

The illustrations for this book were executed in gouache on Strathmore 500 drawing paper.
The text was set in 16/20-point Garamond.

All rights reserved.
For information about permission to reproduce selections from this book,
write to Permissions, Houghton Mifflin Company,
215 Park Avenue South, New York, NY 10003.

Printed in the USA

Library of Congress Cataloging-in-Publication Data

Joosse, Barbara M.
The morning chair / by Barbara M. Joosse ; illustrated by Marcia Sewall.
p.   cm.
Summary: Bram and his family leave their small brick house
in Holland and travel to a new life in New York City.
ISBN 0-395-62337-5
[1. Emigration and immigration—Fiction. 2. Dutch Americans—Fiction.
3. New York (N.Y.)—Fiction.] I. Sewall, Marcia, ill. II. Title.
PZ7.J7435Mo   1995
[E]—dc20   93-4870
                                                      CIP
                                                      AC

WOZ   10   9   8   7   6   5   4   3   2   1

For Sari,
who taught me about sharing chairs,
and for John, Addy, Pete, and Bill,
who shared them.
—B.M.J.

For littlest Edgar.
—M.S.

Bram lived in a small brick house in the middle of a crooked street in a seaside village in Holland.

On Sundays, Bram and Papa took a walk to the sea. Many people knew them and they waved to Bram along the way. Papa bought raw herring from a little stand with a striped awning, and they dipped the small fish in chopped onions and ate them.

"Ah!" they said together.

At night Bram slept in his own little bed, on a straw mattress, tucked in tight with Oma's quilt.

In the mornings, Bram and Mama snuggled up in the morning chair. Mama poured tea from a blue-and-white pot. She put milk into Bram's tea, so it would taste better.

Together they listened to the old clock ticking and the soft sounds of their neighbors outside the window.

Sometimes they talked about America.

"What's America like?" asked Bram.

"It's big, much bigger than Holland.

There are mountains and black bears and coyotes."

"What else?"

"There are cowboys in ten-gallon hats and silver spurs."

"What else?"

"Some people say there are green olives for every meal, and usually steak. There are tall houses with elevators," Mama said, "and maybe a job for Papa."

On June 14, 1950 they received their immigration papers for
America. Everything was packed into wooden crates—Bram's
clackety scooter, his bed with the straw mattress, the old clock,
Mama's silver tea spoons, Papa's pipes . . . and the morning chair.
On their way to the ship Bram held Papa's hand tightly

because he didn't want to lose him. Papa kept patting his pockets, to make sure the passports and immigration papers were still there. Mama kept counting the luggage, to make sure they hadn't lost any. When they passed a herring stand, they were too busy to stop.

Mama and Papa practiced their new language, English, with the other passengers. They talked about jobs and apartments and subways and all the other things they would find in America.

In the ship's dining room, little dishes of green olives were at each table. Bram had never seen a green olive.

"Eat some olives, Bram," said Papa. "They are American."

Bram tried one. It made his mouth squeeze together.

"I don't like green olives," he said.

"Americans love to eat olives," Mama said.

"But I'm Dutch!" said Bram.

No one listened to Bram, and they made him eat green olives anyway.

Papa was the first to see the shore of America. There was the Statue of Liberty! The passengers were quiet, and some of them cried a little. Mama explained that sometimes people cry when they are happy.

After Mama and Papa and Bram passed through immigration, they took a taxi to their new apartment in New York. The apartment was small and empty. They had to eat and sleep on the floor because their furniture hadn't arrived yet.

America was fast and noisy. Cars honked, sirens howled, and people looked at their feet and not at Bram. Everyone spoke English, and Bram couldn't understand them. There were no cowboys and there were no mountains.

Mama took Bram shopping in a big supermarket. A lot of the food was different from Holland, the money was different, and the language was new. So Mama didn't have time to talk to Bram while she shopped.

Papa found a job in a factory. He got up early, before Bram was awake, and he came home late, just before Bram went to sleep.

Bram missed Holland! He missed the brick house and friendly
neighbors and walks with Papa to the sea. He missed his clackety
scooter and his little bed with the straw mattress and Oma's quilt.
Most of all, Bram missed time with Mama in the morning chair.

But Sundays were nice. Mama and Papa and Bram walked to the park. They bought hot dogs with mustard from a little stand with a striped umbrella. They threw pieces of bun to the birds. And Bram took turns with Mama and Papa on the teeter-totter.

It was a happy day when the furniture came.
Papa and Mama unloaded the crates.
"Can I help?" Bram asked Papa.
Papa was busy ripping open the crates, and he didn't hear.
"Where's the morning chair?" asked Bram, more loudly.
Mama looked at all the crates. "I don't know, Bram," she said.

That night, Bram slept on his own little bed with the straw mattress, covered with Oma's quilt. He slept with his nose to the straw and he breathed it in. It smelled like Holland!

But Bram's dreams were of honking cars and sirens and crowds of people, not of Holland. The people had wheels on their legs and they lived in tall, skinny houses with elevators. The people zoomed so fast on their wheel-legs that Bram couldn't see their faces.

Bram woke up with a lonely, hole-in-his-stomach feeling.
He went into the living room in his pajamas . . . and there
was the morning chair!

"Bram," Mama said, "do you know what time it is?"

Bram pulled his breath from the soles of his feet, and let it out slowly.

"It's time for the morning chair," he said. He crawled into the morning chair, jiggled his legs, and waited.

Mama poured tea from the blue-and-white pot. Then she added milk and sugar to Bram's, so it would taste better. She passed a plate of *speculaas*.

Bram held the flat, spicy cookie that was shaped like a windmill. He stuck one finger through the tiny hole, the window in the windmill. Then he plucked one of the almonds out of the cookie and ate that first.

"Mama," said Bram, "I thought America would have cowboys and mountains."

"There are cowboys and mountains in America, but not in New York City. But here there are tall buildings with elevators."

"And green olives!" said Bram.

"In America, there are many kinds of food, and people eat what they like. To tell you the truth, Bram, I don't like olives either. They taste too sour."

"Yes," said Bram. "They're too sour and too green."

"Then you and I don't have to eat them anymore," said Mama.

Bram nibbled at his *speculaas* while he thought. "Mama, there are policemen on horses in America," he said. "I like that."

"Me, too," said Mama.

MASSAN ... NAL LIBRARY
DISCARD
Harrisonburg, VA 22801

Bram looked around the room at the Holland things.
Then he looked at Mama and smiled.
"And there's you and me in the morning chair!"
Mama smoothed Bram's hair off his forehead. "Bram," she said,

"America is a big, big place. There's room for mountains and cowboys and taxis. There's room for people who like green olives, and for people who don't. Most of all, there's room for us and there's room for the morning chair."

Bram took a sip of his tea with milk. Then Mama and Bram listened to the old clock ticking. They listened to the cars whooshing, dogs barking, and taxis honking. They listened to the laughing and talking of the people outside their window, their new neighbors in America.